First American Edition 2010
by Kane Miller, A Division of EDC Publishing
Tulsa, Oklahoma

First published in Great Britain by HarperCollins Children's Books in 2010
Text and illustrations copyright © Jez Alborough 2010

For information contact:
Kane Miller, A Division of EDC Publishing
PO Box 470663
Tulsa, OK 74147-0663
www.kanemiller.com
www.edcpub.com

Library of Congress Control Number: 2009942386
Printed in China
11 12 13 14 15 16 17 18

ISBN: 978-1-935279-66-2

The GOBBLE GOBBLE MOOOOOOO Tractor Book

Jez Alborough

Kane Miller
A DIVISION OF EDC PUBLISHING

For Sue, from Jez

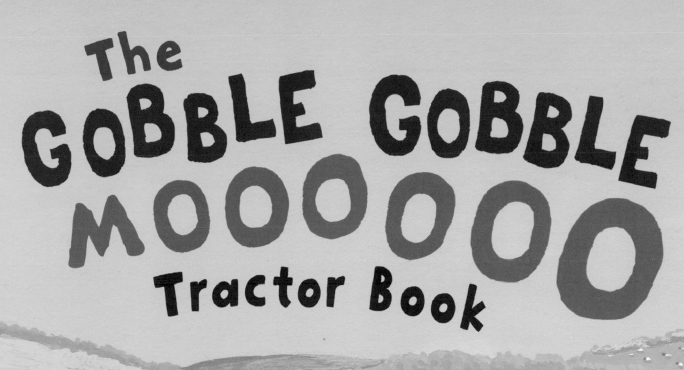

The GOBBLE GOBBLE MOOOOOO Tractor Book

Early one morning,
when Farmer Dougal
was still asleep...

Sheep climbed onto the big red tractor.

"What are you doing?" asked **Cat**.
"I'm going for a ride," said **Sheep**.
"This is the sound the tractor makes
when you turn the engine on..."

"Can I come?" asked **Cat**.
"I can do the sound the engine makes
when it starts to wiggle and jiggle..."

PURRR

"Let's do it again," said **Cat**.
"But what about Farmer Dougal?" asked **Sheep**.
"What if he wakes up and sees us?"

GOBBLE

Cat and **Turkey** looked at **Sheep**
with two silly smirks and said,

P·L·E·A·S·E

"It's wiggling and jiggling..."

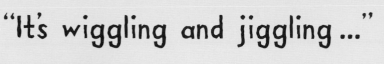

PURRRRR

"And the tractor is driving off down the lane..."

GOBBLE GOBBLE

GOBBLE GOBBLE

"Can I come too?" asked Mouse. "I can do the wheels! The great big wheels which go round and round with a ..."

SQUEAK SQUEAK SQUEAK

"Wait for me!" said **Goose**. "I can do the horn, which shouts, 'Get out of the way!' with a ..."

Honk Honk Honk

"I can do the engine when the tractor goes fast," said **Cow**.
"It gets louder and louder
and sounds like this..."

MoOOOOOOO!

"Let's do it again!" said **Cat**.
"We can all join in," said Mouse.

"But what about Farmer Dougal?" asked **Sheep**.

Then **Cat**, **Turkey**, Mouse, **Goose** and **Cow**
looked at **Sheep** with five soppy smiles and said ...

P·L·E·A·S·E

"All right," said **Sheep**. "Ready ...

SOMEONE IS DRIVING OFF WITH MY TRACTOR!

"QUICK!" cried Sheep. "It's Farmer Dougal..."

Farmer Dougal looked out of the window...
and there was his big red tractor, safe and sound.

"I must have been dreaming," he said.
Then he pulled the curtains shut and climbed
back into bed.

Then **Cow** looked at **Sheep**,

Turkey looked at **Sheep**,

Mouse looked at **Sheep**,

Cat looked at **Sheep**,

Goose looked at **Sheep**,

and **Sheep** looked at them all with a big, goofy grin and said...